Spooksville

Return of the Dead

Christopher Pike

Hodder
Children's
Books

a division of Hodder Headline plc

Copyright © 1997 Christopher Pike

First published in Great Britain in 1997
by Hodder Children's Books
a division of Hodder Headline plc
338 Euston Road
London NW1 3BH

A Catalogue record for this book is available from the British Library

ISBN 0 340 68628 6

Typeset by Avon Dataset Ltd, Bidford-on-Avon, Warks

Printed and bound in Great Britain by
Mackays, Chatham, Kent.

One

Adam Freeman and Watch were walking home late one evening past Spooksville's graveyard when the first of the dead awoke and attacked them. It was ironic that Adam and his friend were talking about death just before the bony creature appeared. Of course later they were to understand that it was no coincidence at all that the skeleton attacked when it did.

There is a reason people often hush their words when they walk past a cemetery after dark. Even the dead have ears, so the stories say, and in Spooksville they have been known to hear even whispers.

1

Specifically, what Adam and Watch were talking about was Watch's return from the dead. During a dangerous quest in another dimension, Watch had died. He had been cursed by a prince acting as a wizard and then had laid down his life to save a princess. Watch's friends had taken his body back to Spooksville and buried him in Spooksville's cemetery. But just as they were saying their final goodbyes, Watch had walked up. Naturally when they saw him they almost all fainted because they had just put him in the ground.

'Now I understand that you are a *second* Watch,' Adam said as he picked up what had happened from that point. Adam was intelligent and fond of solving riddles. On the short side, with brown hair and brown eyes, he had earned a reputation for being very brave. Adam continued, 'But what I don't understand is how the *first* Watch could come back in time to *this* time when he went to the other time also.'

'You are confused,' Watch said in a tone that was friendly and not the least condescending. Watch was considered to be the group genius. He was bigger than Adam and well muscled, yet he could hardly see and was somewhat clumsy. He appeared to live alone in a strange house filled with gadgets. No one knew his real name; he was called Watch because he always wore four watches at the same time. Watch continued, 'After we found the Time Toy and travelled back and forth in time, and messed everything up, we decided that the only way we could fix things was to make it so we had never found the Time Toy in the first place. I volunteered to return in time to just the moment before the toy was found. When I came to that time, there was already a Watch then. I had to be careful to avoid him, to avoid all of you. But once I took the toy away, all the adventures we had with the toy never happened. That is why you can't remember them.'

'But you still haven't answered my question,' Adam said.

'Then I am not sure what you are trying to ask.'

Adam scratched his head. 'I'm not sure either. But it seems to me if the adventures never happened, then there shouldn't have been two of you when everything was said and done. Everything should have been put back to normal.'

'Everything was put back to normal except when it came to me,' Watch said. 'I was the wild element, the ingredient X in the time travel equation.'

'So since that night there have been two of you in Spooksville?'

'I wasn't here all the time. I went down to Los Angeles for a while.'

'What did you try to do there?' Adam asked.

'Get a job at Jet Propulsion Laboratories. They said I was too young.'

'It must have been lonely for you not being able to talk to us,' Adam continued.

Watch hesitated. 'I am used to being alone.'

'Did the other Watch, the one who died, know about you?'

Watch considered. 'No. I don't see how he could have. But when I was in town, and spying on you guys, I saw him suddenly glance over his shoulder a few times. Like he knew someone was watching him.'

4

Adam nodded. 'There must have been some kind of psychic link there. I mean you were the same guy. Was it weird seeing yourself?'

Watch sighed. 'Yeah. It was really weird.'

'Did you ever bump into one of us?'

Watch paused. 'Yeah.'

'Who?' Adam asked.

Watch smiled. 'I bumped into you once, at the movie theatre. We saw *The Return of the Space Worms* together.'

'That was *you?*'

'That was me. You must have never talked to Watch about it later. If you had, he would have been confused. I don't think he saw it.'

Adam was thoughtful. 'Now that you mention it, neither of us liked it so it never came up in conversation again.'

'For the most part I was careful to stay out of the way. But when you were fighting the vampires, I did help you without your knowledge. I drove off a couple that were about to attack you guys just before you returned to the hospital and discovered that

Cindy had been turned into a vampire.'

'How did you drive them off?' Adam asked.

Watch looked away, in the direction of the cemetery. It was coming up on their left, as was the witch's castle. Adam wondered what it was like for his friend to walk past the place where he had been buried – once. In the fading evening light, the graveyard looked haunted. The bare-branched trees hung over the cracked and toppled headstones like bony arms. Yet Adam blinked as he stared at the place. He thought he saw something moving inside. No, he thought, that was impossible. No one would go into the cemetery so late.

'I would rather not say,' Watch answered finally.

Adam studied his friend, suspecting what his friend was getting at. 'Where is the Time Toy now?'

Watch lowered his head and repeated himself. 'I would rather not say.'

It was then they noticed the man walking towards them, on the other side of the road, closer to the cemetery. He was about thirty years old, dressed in a suit and tie, and carrying a black briefcase. Adam did not know his name but recognized him from a bank downtown where Adam had a bank account. The man noticed them and raised his arm in a friendly wave. Adam and Watch went to wave back when they saw a figure suddenly leap over the cemetery wall and land behind the man.

It was dark, they could not see the figure clearly.

But he did not look human.

The thing attacked the man from behind.

'Help!' the man screamed.

Adam and Watch raced across the street and leapt on the back of the figure as it tried to choke the man. They were both horrified to discover that they were trying to tackle a skeleton. The creature was covered with the tattered remains of a blue uniform. He also wore a blue cap, through which poked portions of his white skull. He was so decayed, so empty of flesh, that he didn't smell at all. But his empty eyes as he turned and stared at them over his shoulder chilled them both to the bone. With a whip of his arm, he knocked them both off his back and on to the ground. For a creature who didn't have any muscles, he sure was strong.

Adam and Watch scampered to their feet.

'What should we do?' Adam shouted as he kept his eyes on the creature. It appeared to pause, caught between the three of them glancing this way and that. Its skull was not perfectly formed; there was a small round hole in the temple area. The man from the bank had regained his balance and was watching it from behind. Actually, he was shaking in terror.

'Don't let it kill you,' Watch said.

'Help!' the man screamed. 'Somebody please help us!'

'Crying for help doesn't work in this town, mister,' Adam said. 'We're the best you're going to get.'

The skeleton stopped its fidgeting and focused on Watch. It held out a long bony arm, pointing a finger that looked like a white knife. It worked its creaky jaw and a faint sound seemed to come through its bony ribs and out of its ruined skull.

'*You*,' it hissed.

Then it attacked Watch.

Adam knew another direct attack on the skeleton would be useless, at least without a weapon. Clearly the creature was stronger than a human. Desperately, Adam searched the area for a good strong stick. The man in the suit was hopeless. He seemed to go into shock as the skeleton wrestled Watch to the ground and slowly began to choke the life out of him.

Finally Adam saw what he was looking for, a firm branch lying against the wall of the cemetery. Running for it, he came back swinging, smacking the creature directly over the head as Watch gasped in pain. The blow staggered the skeleton; it fell forward on to Watch, choking him not with its hands this time, but with its gangly form. Adam smacked it again for good measure and then tried to kick it off his friend. Watch was still gasping for breath; he wasn't able to come to Adam's aid. Unfortunately, the blows had only jolted the skeleton. It recovered quickly and jumped back to its feet.

'Mister!' Adam shouted as he readied his stick for

another blow. 'I could really use your help right now!'

The man trembled. 'What can I do?' he mumbled.

The skeleton hissed and descended on Adam.

To Adam, it looked all of ten feet tall.

'Something!' Adam howled as he swung and jumped back at the same time. This time Adam missed; his blow swung wide. The man did not come to his rescue, but Watch did. Even though he was still on the ground and catching his breath, Watch managed to reach out and grab the skeleton's right foot. His grip was weak; it slipped right away. But his effort was enough to trip the skeleton as it tried to grab Adam. Rather than having the skeleton all over him, Adam had the creature kneeling in front of him. Adam did not waste the opportunity. He held up the stick above his head and then delivered another strong blow to the skeleton's skull. This time he smacked it from the side, hard too, real hard. Yet even Adam was surprised when the skeleton's head went flying off the creature's shoulders.

The white skull landed in the bushes.

The rest of the skeleton lay down on the sidewalk and was still.

Adam stepped over the body and helped his friend to his feet.

'Thanks,' Watch said as he brushed himself off. 'For a moment there I thought I was a goner.'

'You're the one who tripped it up,' Adam said as he set down the stick.

'Help!' the man suddenly screamed as he turned and bolted out of sight.

'And thank you!' Adam yelled after him. He shook his head as he stared down at the headless skeleton. 'The adults in this town – they just don't know how to deal with the reality of this place.'

'They have lost their imagination,' Watch agreed. 'When horror appears, they freeze up.' He poked the skeleton with his shoe. 'I wonder why this guy woke back up in such a bad mood.'

Adam knelt by the remains. 'Could he have been exposed to some weird kind of cosmic radiation like in that famous horror movie?'

11

Watch knelt beside him. 'I suppose it's possible. But I would think that would have woken up all the skeletons.'

Adam glanced over the stone wall at the cemetery. 'How do we know more are not about to wake up?'

Watch followed his line of sight. 'We really should check out the place.'

Adam swallowed and glanced around. The shadows had lengthened and covered the city. It was now virtually dark.

'Do you think there would be any harm in waiting until tomorrow morning to check out the place?' Adam said.

Watch laughed softly. 'No harm as long as another dozen skeletons don't wake up in the middle of the night and attack the city.' He paused and rubbed his neck. 'I am kind of beat up right now. I don't mind waiting until tomorrow.'

'Good.' Adam picked up the police cap that had fallen off the skeleton. 'I wonder who he was.'

Watch stood and continued to rub his neck.

'I wonder why he attacked me.'

Adam stood and patted his friend on the back. There had been an odd note in Watch's voice. One of fear, actually, which Watch seldom showed.

'He wasn't after you in particular,' Adam said. 'He's a dead man – he just hates living people in general.'

Watch glanced at the dark cemetery. There was no further sign of movement but it seemed as if the place no longer rested so easily.

'I wonder,' Watch muttered.

Two

The next morning, Adam and Watch had breakfast at their favourite doughnut shop with the rest of the gang. Cindy Makey and Sally Wilcox were there, along with Bryce Poole. Like Adam, Cindy was relatively new to town. She had not grown up in Spooksville like Sally, Bryce and Watch. She was still surprised when the supernatural reared its ugly head and tried to kill them. Yet Cindy was far from a coward, and had often saved the day by her daring and quick thinking. She had blonde hair and a sweet face and was secretly in love with Adam.

Sally was tough and smart. She had seen so

many scary creatures in her twelve short years that nothing fazed her any more. In a sense she was kind of scary herself. Her wit was so sharp the others never knew what she was going to come up with next. Yet Sally was also very resourceful. She may have often got them into trouble, but just as often she had got them out of trouble. Skinny and tall, she had long dark hair and a habit of talking even in her sleep.

Bryce Poole was a young James Bond. His purpose in life seemed to be to keep the world from being destroyed. Although he had a habit of taking himself too seriously, from time to time, the others had grown to trust him. Bryce had short dark hair and a handsome face that could look remarkably innocent when he smiled, which was seldom.

Over milk and doughnuts, Adam and Watch explained about the attack of the skeleton. Sally and Bryce listened with calm interest, but Cindy was horrified. She made a face as the boys finished their story.

'This is impossible,' she said, perhaps trying to

convince herself. 'The dead cannot return to life. It's not natural.'

'Like we live in the natural capital of the world,' Sally muttered.

'Natural laws do not apply in Spooksville,' Bryce told Cindy. 'That's what makes it such an interesting place to live.'

'I do not find murderous skeletons interesting,' Cindy said.

'It may not have been trying to kill me,' Watch said.

'When you choke someone real hard, you're usually trying to kill them,' Sally said.

'The real question is why did the skeleton suddenly come back to life,' Bryce said. 'And are more of the skeletons going to attack?'

'I agree,' Adam said. 'We have to get at the cause of this attack. We need to get to the cemetery and examine the evidence.'

'What did you guys do with the remains of the skeleton?' Bryce asked.

'Left it where it fell,' Adam said. 'I mean, I

17

couldn't take the bones home. How could I explain them to my parents?'

'I want to go roller blading,' Sally complained. 'I don't want to go to the cemetery. It's a dirty place – I don't want to catch something.'

'Would you rather just turn your head and pretend this never happened?' Bryce asked.

'As I get older and wiser about this town, I see there is a lot of reason to adopt such a strategy,' Sally said.

'I don't mind going to the cemetery as long as I know what we're looking for,' Cindy said.

'We're just looking for anything odd,' Bryce said.

Sally smiled. 'We can look in a mirror if that's all we want.'

Adam glanced at Watch, who seemed to be thinking.

'What's the matter?' Adam asked.

'Nothing,' Watch said.

'How's the throat?' Adam asked.

Watch touched his throat. 'It hurts a little, it's no big deal.'

Sally studied him as well. 'But something's bothering you.'

Watch shrugged and stood up. 'Let's check out the cemetery. We need more facts.'

In the bright sunshine, Spooksville's graveyard seemed less scary. As they entered through the wrought iron gates and looked around, the place appeared almost peaceful. Of course the cemetery was not unfamiliar to them. It was here that they had entered the Secret Path, through Madeline Templeton's giant tombstone, that strange magical portal into other dimensions. On the whole the cemetery had actually been a useful place for them in the past. Yet today, even though everything looked normal, they knew that something was deeply wrong with Spooksville's resident corpses.

'I don't see anything. Let's go,' Sally said.

'We just got here,' Cindy said.

'It is never wise to overstay one's welcome at a cemetery,' Sally warned.

They had already searched the sidewalk outside

the cemetery for signs of the skeleton's bones. But they were gone. They did not know if someone from town had picked them up or if the skeleton had somehow put himself back together and crawled away.

'We need to search for any dug-up graves,' Bryce said as he stepped forward into the cemetery. He had, in fact, brought a shovel with him. Not that any of them were asking what he planned to do with it.

'That's sick,' Sally said.

'If we find one it will be even more sick,' Bryce warned.

They found one a few minutes later, in the far corner of the cemetery. The ground was disturbed and the tombstone had toppled over. Watch turned it back over and studied the information on it.

'William Smith,' he said. 'He died only three years ago.'

'What did he die of?' Sally asked.

'They don't generally list such information on a tombstone,' Cindy muttered.

'In this town I think they should,' Sally said.

'Does it matter what he died of?' Bryce said.

'It might,' Adam said grimly.

Watch frowned as he stared down at the mangled earth.

'I wonder if he crawled back underground,' he said.

Bryce held up his shovel. 'Should we dig him back up?'

No one looked too excited about that idea.

'What time exactly did this William attack you guys?' Sally asked.

'It was not long after sunset,' Adam said.

'Interesting,' Sally muttered.

Watch nodded. 'The skeletons may be allergic to the sun, like vampires.'

Cindy looked worried. 'You say skeletons plural. I don't see any more disturbed graves.'

'We have to assume the worst,' Bryce said. 'I think we need to stake this place out this evening at sunset.'

Watch agreed. 'But let's see what we can find out

21

about this William Smith.' Then he added, 'And why he came after me.'

They headed to the public library, where Mr Spiney worked. Mr Spiney was really into people's bones. Rumour had it that he collected them – from dead people – in his closet at home. Certainly, whenever some kid went into the library, he always asked about his or her bones, and whether they were drinking enough milk. Mr Spiney looked kind of bony himself. Dressed all in black and bent over like some kind of skeleton, he looked like an under-taker who couldn't get enough business. But the gang didn't really mind him. They thought he con-tributed to the local colour of the town.

Mr Spiney met them at the door of the library.

'Hello, children, and welcome,' he said, as he always did. 'I do hope your hands are clean and your minds are not dirty. Would you like a glass of milk?'

'No, thank you,' Adam said. 'We're here just to check out your old newspapers.'

22

'Adam Freeman,' Mr Spiney said as he peered at Adam. He leaned over and felt Adam's shoulder. 'I do believe you're getting a slouch.'

'Look who's talking,' Sally muttered.

Mr Spiney glanced at her. 'And how are you, Sally Wilcox? Have you had your milk today? You know you can never get enough calcium. Doctors everywhere say that strong bones are essential. Once you're dead, that's all you have left. You don't want to be slouching in your own coffin.' He added darkly, 'Or wherever your bones end up.'

Sally forced a sweet smile. 'When I die I'm going to have myself cremated. That way perverts like you won't even have a chance to steal my bones.'

Mr Spiney looked more horrified than offended. He put his long nails to his mouth and chewed on them nervously.

'You wouldn't burn up such lovely bones, would you?' he asked. 'Without understanding how useful they can be to others?'

'What do you do with all the bones you collect?' Bryce asked.

Now Mr Spiney looked offended.

'Who said that I collect bones?' he asked.

'Well you certainly don't collect stamps,' Sally muttered.

Bryce shrugged. 'It's just a rumour that we've all heard a thousand times over.'

Mr Spiney's eyes brightened. 'What else do people say about me?'

Bryce frowned. 'You don't want to know.'

Mr Spiney turned away. 'Do you want to see back copies of the *Daily Disaster*?' That was Spooksville's local paper. The obituary section took up half of every issue.

'We want issues that are three years old,' Watch said as he followed the librarian.

'May I ask what you are looking for?' Mr Spiney said.

'A subject very close to your heart,' Sally muttered.

Mr Spiney fetched them the issues that they wanted and then locked them in a back room in the library. Mr Spiney was always worried that someone was going to run off with his reference materials. Of course he again offered them each glasses of milk. Watch was the only one to accept his offer; he said he was thirsty.

They found the obituary for William Smith after twenty minutes of searching. Actually, in the paper, his name was listed as *Captain* William Smith. The short notice said he had died in the line of duty, from a gunshot wound to the head.

'I remember he had a hole in his head,' Adam said.

'Maybe that's why he woke up again,' Sally suggested.

'I don't think so,' Watch said, preoccupied.

'What's on your mind?' Adam asked Watch.

Watch frowned. 'William Smith was a captain in the police force. I find that curious.'

'How so?' Bryce asked.

Watch paused. 'That makes him an authority figure.'

'Which means?' Sally persisted.

Watch was thoughtful. 'I don't know.'

'You don't still think he was after you in particular?' Adam asked.

Watch set aside the paper. 'He did point at me just before he attacked.'

'He did?' Sally asked. 'You guys didn't tell us that.'

'I didn't think it was important,' Adam said.

'I thought the skeleton attacked the man first,' Cindy said.

'He did,' Watch said quickly, as if talking to himself. Then he shook himself and turned towards the door. 'I think we'd better get ready for tonight. I think we're going to see some scary stuff.'

They all hurried to catch up with him.

'What makes you say that?' Sally asked.

'It's just a feeling I get,' Watch said. 'A cold feeling.'

Three

That evening, as the orange sun slowly set into the ocean off Spooksville, the gang huddled in the centre of the cemetery. The temperature was not unusually cold and yet they each felt chilly. It was as if an unseen cloud of arctic vapour had settled over the graveyard. Each of them felt as if something awful were about to happen.

'I don't know why we have to do this,' Sally said as she passed in front of the group. 'I mean, it's not like we're getting paid for playing graveyard security guards.'

'Our compensation is knowing deep in our

hearts that we are making the world safe to live in,' Bryce said.

Sally snorted. 'That kind of satisfaction isn't going to put food on our tables, or high-priced designer clothes in our closets.'

'Shh,' Cindy said. 'The more you talk, the better chance is that they will hear us.'

Sally stopped. 'Who will hear us?'

Cindy was nervous. 'The dead.'

'But you don't believe the dead can come back to life?' Sally said.

Cindy glanced around. 'I do right now.'

A cold breeze swept through the cemetery. Overhead the few dead leaves on the brown branches rustled like metal chains being shaken in a haunted castle. To the north, not far away, they could see Ann Templeton's stone castle. A red fiery glow was coming from the highest tower. They each wondered if the witch was watching them, as she often seemed to do during times of danger.

The sun set. The darkness grew.

They huddled closer to each other, and spoke in whispers.

They heard a faint moaning sound.

'What was that?' Cindy gasped.

'I didn't hear anything,' Sally said quickly.

'You did too,' Cindy said.

'Shh,' Sally snapped. 'Don't let it hear you.'

Adam glanced around. 'I think the sound came from the back corner.'

'But not the same corner as William Smith's grave,' Watch said.

'Great,' Sally said. 'Let's run the other way.'

Bryce had his shovel in his hand, and was holding it up like a weapon. 'We're not running anywhere. If a corpse wakes up, we are dealing with it here and now, before it can attack the town.' He glanced in the direction of the back corner. 'I think I see a movement.'

'You're imagining it,' Sally whispered.

'I see something as well,' Watch said, peering through his thick glasses.

'Oh no,' Sally cried.

They heard the moaning sound again, followed by sounds of scraping and moving earth. Yet none of them advanced towards the sound. Even Bryce, who spoke so bravely, stayed exactly where he was. They were a courageous group, but they were also scared out of their minds.

'What should we do?' Adam whispered.

'Run,' Sally said.

'Kill it,' Bryce said.

'But it's already dead!' Sally hissed.

'Can you talk to a corpse?' Cindy asked anxiously.

'What would a corpse have to talk about?' Sally wanted to know.

'The corpse spoke last night,' Watch said.

'What did it say?' Bryce asked.

'It pointed at Watch and said, "*You*,"' Adam said.

'You didn't tell us that either,' Sally complained.

'We didn't want to scare you,' Watch said.

'Oh brother,' Sally gasped.

Bryce was impatient. He strained his eyes in the

poor light. 'If a skeleton is digging its way out of the ground right now, we should attack it before it is totally free. It should be more vulnerable at this point.'

'I agree,' Watch said. 'What do you guys think?'

There was definitely something moving, low down in the ground, over in the far corner of the cemetery. They heard another soul-chilling moan.

'I don't agree with any of this,' Sally protested.

Adam spoke with authority as he took a step towards the monster.

'Let's get it now before it gets us,' he said.

They moved towards the disturbed grave site. There was now no question – there was definitely something trying to dig its way out from beneath the ground. They trembled as they approached, holding on to each other for support. They had faced many horrors in their days in Spooksville but there was something totally unnerving about a creature that could come back from the dead. Closing to within ten feet of the grave, they saw a bony white hand stick out of the earth and grab at a handful of mud.

They almost jumped out of their own skins.

'Quick!' Sally howled. 'Hit it, Bryce!'

The hand vanished.

'I have to wait till it raises its head above the ground,' Bryce said, standing ready with the shovel.

'We should have each brought more weapons,' Adam said.

The ground continued to squirm in front of them.

Yet they saw no more of the skeleton.

'We have to get closer to the grave if we're going to catch it by surprise,' Watch said.

'Are you crazy?' Sally asked. 'What if it grabs us and pulls us under?'

'That won't happen,' Bryce said.

Sally screeched like she was about to die. 'It's got me!'

They glanced over to see that the creature had indeed grabbed hold of Sally's ankle. Before they could react it tugged on her and half her leg disappeared into the moist earth. Sally fell and clawed desperately at the ground.

'Don't let it eat me!' she cried.

They grabbed hold of her in a second but the pull of the underground monster was fierce. The more they tugged to pull her free, the more Sally screamed.

'It's chewing on my leg!' she cried.

'Are you sure?' Adam asked desperately.

'It's doing something disgusting to me!' Sally yelled.

The skeleton pulled harder.

Sally disappeared up to her waist.

'No!' she screamed.

'It's too strong!' Adam shouted as he tried to hang on to Sally's right arm. Bryce and Watch were on her left side, and Cindy was hanging on to Sally's head. But try as they might, they could not keep her from sinking deeper into the ground. Adam added, 'There must be more than one of them!'

'I don't think so,' Watch said. 'I just think it's real strong.'

'Save me!' Sally moaned as she sunk up to her chest.

'We have to dig her out!' Bryce yelled.

'You'll never be able to dig fast enough!' Watch yelled. He glanced at the grave they had been approaching when Sally had been grabbed. 'I have to let go of her! Give me the shovel!'

'Don't let go!' Sally cried.

But Watch did let go of her, and took Bryce's shovel. Rather than trying to dig around the spot where Sally was being pulled down, however, Watch leapt towards the grave and began to dig furiously. Here the ground was loose, probably from the skeleton's trying to claw its way out. In fact there wasn't much soil. Watch was down to the coffin in a few minutes. Unfortunately by that time Sally was buried up to her neck.

'Don't let it kill me!' Sally pleaded.

Cindy yanked on Sally's hair. 'We won't let it get you!' she cried.

Sally groaned in pain. 'And don't make me bald!'

Watch raised the blade of the shovel and drove it hard into the muddy box. Apparently the creature didn't like anyone messing with its home. The grip on Sally suddenly loosened and a second later Watch was thrashing in the hole that he had just dug. Adam jumped up.

'We have to save Watch!' he shouted.

'Save me first and then save him!' Sally yelled, only her head left showing. Cindy and Bryce continued to try to pull Sally out of the ground, but Adam jumped into the grave with his friend. Watch had already lost hold of the shovel, but Adam grabbed it and began to pound the unseen head of the skeleton. They heard a cracking sound which they hoped was the skeleton's skull. For a moment the chaos seemed to stop. Adam was able to help Watch to his feet and Bryce and Cindy were able to pull Sally out of the ground. Just as they were congratulating themselves on their escape, however, the centre of the grave suddenly exploded in a shower of mud and dirt.

Standing before them was a large skeleton.

This one also had on a tattered blue uniform.

It pointed a bony finger at Watch.

'*You,*' it hissed. '*Come.*'

Bryce grabbed the shovel from Adam and held it over his head.

'You,' Bryce said. 'Go!'

Bryce whacked at the skeleton's head and sent its skull flying into the bushes. The remainder of the skeleton collapsed in a lifeless pile. Cautiously the gang stepped to the edge of the grave and stared down at the bones. Watch knelt by the pile and fingered the uniform.

'Another cop,' he whispered.

Adam knelt beside him. 'What does it mean?'

Watch sighed. 'It pointed at me again.'

'No,' Adam said quickly.

'Yeah, it did,' Sally said as she continued to brush the mud off her trousers. Then she let out a screech. 'Oh no!'

They jumped. They searched for another clawing hand.

'What is it?' Bryce demanded. 'Has another one got you?'

'No,' Sally said miserably as she bent over. 'But

36

it scratched me. Look, my leg is bleeding. It has infected me.'

'Does that mean you're going to turn into a flesh-eating corpse like the monsters under the ground?' Cindy asked.

Sally glared at her. 'Show a little tact please.'

Cindy shrugged. 'I just remember when I was changing into a vampire you were the first one who wanted to put a stake through my heart.'

'Bryce wanted to as well,' Sally protested.

'You may be infected,' Bryce said grimly. 'You might turn into one of them.'

Sally was close to weeping. 'I am so glad I have such wonderful friends.'

Adam studied the wound. It looked like an ordinary scratch to him.

'I don't think he bit you,' he said. 'I just think your skin got caught on a weed or something.'

'That's easy for you to say,' Sally said, and she really did look miserable. She kept trying to rub away the scratch but it only made the bleeding worse. 'I need a doctor,' she moaned.

Bryce nodded. 'It might be better to have the leg amputated. Just in case the infection does turn you into a flesh-eating zombie.'

Sally stared at him in shock. 'But it's my leg.'

'If you do get it amputated,' Cindy said, 'I am sure Jaws would take you to the high-school prom when we get older.' Jaws was a nickname for a kid who had lost his leg to a great white shark off Spooksville's coast. Cindy's remark did nothing to soothe Sally. Her moans started to turn to tears.

'I don't want to lose my leg,' she wept. 'I don't want to be a zombie.'

Adam grabbed her shoulders. 'Sally, look at me. Listen to me. Your leg is scratched, nothing more. You're going to be fine.'

Sally looked so sad. 'Really? I don't know.'

Cindy patted Sally on the back. 'I was just teasing you. I'm sure Adam is right and it's just a scratch.'

'But I'd have the leg removed anyway,' Bryce said.

'Would you shut up,' Adam snapped at him.

'This might not be the ideal place to argue,'

Watch said. 'More of these skeletons might wake up. We'd better get out of here, get help.'

'Who's going to help us?' Adam asked. 'Who would believe us?'

'The guy who works at the bank?' Cindy suggested.

'No,' Watch said, and his gaze went to the witch's castle. 'We need to talk to Ann Templeton.'

Bryce was uncertain. 'She told us that we can't go running to her every time we have a little problem.'

'I would call this more than a little problem,' Sally cried as she rubbed at her scratched leg some more. Adam reached over and stopped her.

'You're just making it worse,' he said gently.

Sally nodded weakly. 'I'm just so scared, that's all.'

'You're fine,' Cindy said. 'But if you do get the urge to eat us, please tell us ahead of time.'

Adam sighed and turned back to Watch. 'Why do you think she will help us?'

Watch glanced down at the pile of bones.

'Because we are dealing with something very

deep here,' he said. 'The meaning of life. The meaning of death.' He paused and glanced toward Madeline Templeton's tombstone. But none of them thought it was a coincidence that the earlier version of Watch was buried right next to the old witch. Watch added in a soft voice, 'I hope she will help us.'

Four

Speaking to Ann Templeton seemed their best bet. But Watch was reluctant to leave the graveyard unguarded. Who knew how many other corpses might wake during the night? It was decided that Bryce and Cindy would remain just outside the cemetery and watch for signs of trouble. Neither of them was that close to the town witch anyway.

Nor was Sally a big fan of Ann Templeton. But for once she was anxious to see the witch. Sally hoped Ann Templeton might have a potion that she could rub on her leg to keep her from turning into a zombie. Sally could not talk about anything else on the short hike to the castle.

'I am having strange thoughts,' Sally said as she put a hand to her head.

'What else is new,' Watch muttered.

'I'm serious,' Sally complained. 'Something is happening inside my body. I'm changing.'

'What are you thinking about?' Adam asked.

'Hamburgers,' Sally said.

'That's just because you're hungry,' Adam said.

'But hamburgers are red meat,' Sally said. 'I think it is more than coincidence that I should begin to crave them right now.'

'Do you like hamburgers?' Watch asked.

'I love them,' Sally said. 'You know that.'

Watch smiled. 'Adam's right. You're thinking about them because you're hungry. After we get rid of these skeletons, we can go to McDonalds.'

'Promise?' Sally asked. 'Will you pay?'

Watch lost his smile as he gazed up at the castle.

'I will be happy to pay,' he said.

Somehow his words seemed to have a double meaning.

It was bothering Adam more and more that one form of Watch was buried in the cemetery. Adam imagined that it was bothering Watch as well.

Ann Templeton answered the door of the castle when they knocked. Once again it seemed as if she knew that they were crossing. As always, she was beautiful. Her long dark hair hung down the back of her green robe and her green eyes sparkled like jewels. She led them into a stone room where a huge fireplace crackled with flaming logs. There was a long wooden table in the centre of the room. They had been here before, when they had previously discussed the future of mankind. She offered them a seat at the table and asked if they were thirsty. They all shook their heads. Sally pulled up her trouser leg and showed it to the witch.

'I was scratched by a flesh-eating skeleton,' Sally said. 'Am I going to turn into one?'

Ann Templeton was unconcerned. 'Maybe.'

Sally's face crashed. 'Can you help me?'

Ann Templeton smiled. 'Really, Sally, why should I help you? You don't even like me.'

'That's not true,' Sally said quickly. 'I mean, I have argued with you in the past. I have told people to avoid you, that you were an evil creature and stuff like that. But that doesn't mean I don't like you. I mean, when it comes to witches I've seen much worse.' Sally had to catch her breath. 'Please help me. I hate turning into weird creatures.'

Ann Templeton waved her hand. 'I'll look at it later if you start to behave strangely.'

'But by then it might be too late,' Sally cried.

Ann Templeton ignored her and turned to Watch.

'You look worried,' the witch said gently.

Watch nodded and lowered his head.

'The dead in the cemetery have awoken,' he said.

'I know,' she said.

'We stopped two of them,' Adam said. 'But we think there may be more.'

The witch nodded. 'You can count on that.'

'What do they want?' Adam asked.

Ann Templeton continued to study Watch.

'Do you know what they want?' she asked.

44

Watch drew in a deep breath. He was pale.

'I think they want me,' he said. 'I think they're angry that I cheated death.'

'But I'm the one who has the scratch,' Sally complained.

Adam forced a laugh. 'Watch, you have to be kidding? They're not waking up because of you. It's impossible.'

Ann Templeton was not laughing.

'I have been dreading this day since you walked up to us at your funeral,' she said to Watch. 'I have known there would be an accounting.'

Watch sighed. 'Do I have to die again?'

Ann Templeton spoke carefully. 'Maybe. I wish I knew for sure.'

'Wait a second!' Adam exploded. 'This is not right. Watch is alive. There is nothing wrong with him. There is no reason he has to die.'

Ann Templeton looked at Adam with compassion.

'Adam,' she said. 'You are so brave and yet you look so scared. It is because you do understand what I am saying. When Watch returned to us that day, at his funeral, he upset the balance of life and death. That is not a simple matter. There has to be an accounting.'

Adam shook his head. 'I don't understand. Why does there have to be an accounting? Who's going to make the collection?'

Ann Templeton hesitated. 'The Grim Reaper.'

Adam forced another laugh, boy did he force it.

'That's just a myth,' he said. 'There is no Grim Reaper.'

'And who do you think is commanding the dead to awake?' the witch asked.

'Do I have to meet this guy?' Sally asked. 'Are you sure you don't have some kind of magical potion that I can rub on my leg?'

The other three ignored her.

'What do you know about the Grim Reaper?' Watch asked.

Again she paused. 'I knew someone who met him once. It was my best friend actually, Cio.'

Watch was interested. 'Can you tell us about it?'

'No,' Sally said, trembling. 'Don't tell us. I don't need to hear a story like that right now. Maybe after my leg is better.' She leaned over and examined it. 'Oh no, it's turning a funny colour.'

Ann Templeton considered. 'Maybe Sally is right, maybe this is not the best night for this story. But I feel I should tell you. I feel I owe you that much.'

'Is it a sad story?' Adam asked anxiously.

Ann Templeton had a faraway look in her eyes.

'It's a sad but beautiful story,' she said finally. 'It's about Cio and Sam. I knew them both all my young life. This story takes place when we were all twenty-one. They were the happiest couple, so much in love. They were engaged to be married. Wherever you went in town, you could see them holding hands, kissing, so glad to be near each other. Yet I would say their love was not selfish. It seemed to radiate out from them and fill others. When people saw their happiness they felt happy too.' Ann Templeton paused and a cloud crossed her face. 'The whole town grieved when Sam died.'

47

Adam had to take a breath. 'How did he die?'

Ann Templeton looked up. 'It was nothing mysterious. He was hit by a car. It didn't kill him right away, and that was the terrible thing. For a long time he hung on to life in the hospital, breathing by a mechanical respirator. But after seven days the doctors spoke to Cio and told her that it was hopeless, that his brain was dead. They were keeping alive a vegetable. They wanted her permission to pull the plug. Of course Cio, bless her sensitive heart, wouldn't let them. Cio was still praying for a miracle. You see even though Sam had serious head injuries, he looked just fine. He lay there on the bed and he looked like he was just sleeping. I visited him myself every day.' Her voice grew soft. 'Yeah, every day I sat by his side, by Cio, and thought if only I could heal him. If only I could put my hands on his head and make it so that he would open his eyes and climb out of bed and kiss Cio's tears away.' She stopped and her face seemed old right then. 'But I could not do that for him.'

'Why not?' Adam asked carefully. 'I mean, did

you have the power to do it?' He knew the witch had great healing abilities. He had seen her fix Watch's eyes a couple of times. Yet Ann Templeton shook her head in response to his question.

'I could not do it,' she said simply. 'It was not right. Sam was dead, I knew that in my heart even though his heart continued to beat. There was no help for him. I tried to tell Cio that. She had to listen to the doctors, I said. Let them remove Sam from the respirator, let him die with dignity. But there was no convincing her, and I had to sit there, day after day, and watch as the situation tore her apart. Life is often hard, death is usually painful, but to be caught somewhere in between the two, for anyone, is intolerable. Cio's grief could not heal because she would not let the wound close. She simply could not let Sam go.' Ann Templeton wiped away a tear. They had never seen her cry before. 'She was my best friend and I didn't know what to do to help her.'

They let her sit silently for a moment. Finally she continued.

'It was me who ended it for her. Or so I thought. One afternoon, when Cio was resting in the adjoining room, I reached over and pulled the plug on the respirator. I just killed the power, and then I sat there and watched Sam die. It did not seem such a terrible thing. He looked so much at peace, I was relieved. Yet when I went to wake Cio and tell her that it was over, she did not believe me. The look in her eyes was strange, she did not even get up and check on him. Instead she left the hospital, and no one saw where she went.' Ann Templeton coughed. 'It was only later that I discovered what she did.'

'What was that?' Adam asked, not really wanted to know.

Ann Templeton briefly closed her eyes. 'After she left the hospital she set up camp at the corner of the cemetery. No one saw her. Like I said, I found out this later. But what she planned to do was stop the Grim Reaper when he came to the cemetery for Sam's soul. By the power of her love she thought she could bring Sam back to life. I am sure other grieved people have had such ideas but Cio really meant to do it. The night after we buried Sam, she waited beside his grave. Cio's focus on Sam was so intense it granted her some kind of subtle vision. What I mean is she could see the movement of Sam's ghost, of all creatures in the spirit realm. So that when the Grim Reaper entered the cemetery to collect Sam's soul, Cio was aware. And she stood to block him.'

'How did she do that?' Sally gasped.

Ann Templeton smiled faintly. 'She just did it that's all. Her determination was that great. The Grim Reaper had to stop and listen to her. She said, "You can't have my Sam. He belonged to me, you get out of here." Well, the Grim Reaper is not one to give orders to. He said, "Your fiancé is dead. He died young and before his time but these things happen. Step aside, he belongs to me now." Then Cio did a horrible thing. She offered a deal to the Grim Reaper. She said that she would give up the remainder of her own life if she could have just one more day with Sam. If he would bring him back to her for just twenty-four hours, then she would go with him as well, to wherever the Grim Reaper took human souls.'

'Where's that?' Sally interrupted.

Ann Templeton stared at her. 'You don't want to know.'

'Do I want to know?' Watch asked softly.

She looked at him with love. 'Let me finish my story, maybe their example can help you, I'm not sure.' She paused. 'As I said, Cio made her offer, and the Grim Reaper paused to consider. He is not exactly like people think, he can be bargained with. It is just that his system of accounting never favours a mortal. Cio's proposition intrigued him. He knew Cio was destined to live a long life, but if he could take her at the same time as Sam, then he reasoned that he would have collected the merit of almost an entire human life.'

'It is a great thing to be born as a human being,' Ann Templeton said. 'Cio was offering to exchange that gift for what the Grim Reaper considered to be very little. As a result, the Grim Reaper would inherit the bulk of the gift. Perhaps he would use it later himself, to take birth somewhere, I honestly don't know. But what I do know is that he agreed to Cio's offer. In a flash of dark light he vanished and then Cio heard Sam moaning deep inside his coffin. There was a shovel nearby and she quickly dug him out.'

'Was Sam all right?' Adam asked, fascinated by the story. It was a grim tale but – Ann Templeton was right – it had a sad beauty to it as well. That Cio would sacrifice so much to be with the one she loved. Ann Templeton slowly shook her head even though she answered yes.

'He seemed to be the old Sam,' she said. 'Cio was overjoyed to see him. But Sam was fully alert, and he knew something was not right. He knew he had been dead, and that he shouldn't be on Earth. And when Cio explained to him what she had done, he was horrified. He loved Cio, he didn't want her sacrificing her whole life just to be with him another twenty-four hours. But of course Cio had no intention of keeping her end of the bargain. She wanted to leave Spooksville with Sam, to go and hide in a place where the Grim Reaper would never find them.'

'Is there such a place nearby?' Sally asked nervously, still rubbing at the scratch on her leg.

'That was the fatal flaw in Cio's plan,' Ann Templeton said. 'She knew of no such place. It was only then she came to me, with Sam, and told me what she had done. Naturally I was as upset as Sam. Cio was my best friend, I didn't want to lose her. But I had to do what I could to help her, especially when he begged me to. She was scared, make no mistake about it, yet she thought she could outfox the Grim Reaper. She felt that as her love had been strong enough to stop him the first time, it would stop him again. But she was leaving it up to me to make her plan a practical one.'

'Where did you go?' Sally asked.

Ann Templeton considered 'Guess.'

Watch spoke. 'To the stars.'

Ann Templeton was impressed. 'How did you know?'

'I know you have friends there,' Watch said simply.

'How do you know?' Ann Templeton persisted.

Watch smiled faintly. 'Because you have star dust in your hair.'

Ann Templeton smiled. 'That's very kind of you. And yes, it is true, I have friends out among the stars. And I called to them to come and take Cio, Sam and me away in what you would call a spaceship. My friends arrived in less than twelve hours, and we were many light years from Earth when the Grim Reaper's deadline approached. And for a few hours after that it seemed that Cio's plan had worked because nothing happened. The Grim Reaper did not show, and Sam and Cio seemed perfectly fine. I was so relieved, I went to a private room aboard the spaceship and fell fast asleep. It had, after all, been a long and stressful day. But that was my mistake, if that was my only mistake.'

'What happened?' Adam asked, dying to know. Well, not really dying to but anxious to know. He didn't want to die just then, not after what he was hearing.

Ann Templeton shrugged weakly, and it was unusual for her to show any sign of weakness. She was
always so strong, always in command. The three of
them realized how dear Cio and Sam and must
have been to her.

'I was asleep for only a couple of hours when I
suddenly awoke and knew something was wrong. I
rushed to the room where Cio and Sam were supposed to be sleeping and I found them resting in
each others arms. Only they were not resting, they
were dead. There was not a mark on either of them
but they were no longer breathing, and their skin
was already turning cold. I didn't know how it had
happened, or rather, why it should have happened
after the deadline had passed. But then I noticed
Cio's watch lying beside her head. The arms of the
watch had been pulled up and out of the glass face
plate. Then I understood that it had been the Grim
Reaper who had mangled the watch.'

'Why?' Watch asked.

'He was trying to tell me that when we had
travelled through deep space, we had experienced

time distortion due to our tremendous velocity. In reality he had returned for Cio and Sam right on schedule, only we had thought we had fooled him because more than twenty-four hours had passed on the watches we wore on our wrists. But on Earth time had moved at a different rate. In other words the Grim Reaper had not been fooled. He had collected what he felt was rightfully his exactly on time.'

'You never saw them again?' Adam whispered, knowing what the answer would be. Ann Templeton looked away, to the crackling fire, the red flames. It seemed then as if she felt a chill that no fire could erase.

'No,' she said quietly. 'They were gone. I knew of no power that could bring them back.'

They were silent for a long time. And Adam knew that Ann Templeton would not have told them such a personal story unless it had a bearing on their present situation. She believed the Grim Reaper was preparing for another visit. It was Watch who finally spoke.

'I guess I don't have to ask you why you told us that story,' he said.

She nodded sadly. 'The Grim Reaper does not like to be cheated, and I am sure he thinks you chested him. He was probably on the way to collect your soul when you showed up at your own funeral. All of us thought it was a miracle, and it was a miracle. But I told you, there was a part of me even then that was worried.'

'You have been waiting for something like this to happen?' Watch asked.

'Yes.'

Watch fidgeted. 'I don't suppose you can arrange for me to go for a ride on a spaceship before the Grim Reaper gets here?'

'Is he coming for me too?' Sally moaned.

'He's not coming for anybody,' Adam snapped. He spoke with emotion to Ann Templeton. 'What happened to your friends does not have to repeat itself tonight. Watch made no bargain with the Grim Reaper. He owes him nothing.'

'Yet he did bargain with the Grim Reaper when

58

he offered to sacrifice his life for the princess during your dangerous quest,' Ann Templeton said. 'Once he made that offer, the Grim Reaper was aware. And when Watch's other body died, the Grim Reaper made an appointment to collect him. Yet he couldn't collect him because Watch was up and walking around. So he sent the legions of his dead to get him. And that's what they want, they want to kill Watch.'

Adam felt despair. 'But can't you protect him? You're so powerful.'

Ann Templeton spread her hands. 'I couldn't protect Cio, and she meant more to me than my own life. How can I save Watch?'

Adam's eyes stung with tears. 'There must be something you can do.'

She was silent for a long time. 'I am sorry, I don't know what it is.'

They heard a noise outside, strange hissing sounds.

Ann Templeton stood and stepped to a window.

The others stood as well, although Watch slowly.

He seemed resigned to his fate.

'They're coming for me?' Watch asked quietly.

Ann Templeton turned and stared at him.

'Yes,' she said. 'They are coming.'

Five

Meanwhile, Cindy and Bryce were guarding the cemetery and doing a lousy job. It really was a spooky place to hang out after dark, especially with the bodies digging themselves out of the ground and all, so they had decided to move a discreet distance away: just across the street, where they thought it would be OK to watch. They could still see the graveyard, although probably not as well as they should have been able to. Because they were sitting on the street kerb, the cemetery's stone wall partially blocked their way. Still, they thought they would know if any new monsters were to stir.

They were wrong about that, though.

'How do you feel?' Bryce asked, sitting in the dark beside her, his shovel resting nearby.

'I'm OK,' Cindy said. 'But I'd rather be at home with my kid brother and mother and watching TV.'

'I hear you. This always having to save Spooksville and the world from danger is getting boring.'

Cindy was surprised. 'But I thought that is what you lived for? You know, being a superhero and all. I would think you would get bored without all the action.'

'I don't know. I have been thinking it would be nice to settle down finally.'

'Bryce, you can't be thinking of settling down. You're only twelve years old.'

'I'll be thirteen soon,' he said quickly.

'Still. We're just kids.'

'So what are you saying? That you like running into monsters every other week?'

Cindy shrugged. 'I'm not saying I like it any more than you do. But at least it does keep things interesting. I mean, where I used to live, you never got into outer space or alien dimensions or anything like that. Here it happens all the time.'

'I'm sorry, Cindy, I never pegged you as the adventurous type.'

Cindy smiled. 'Why? Because I'm a coward?'

'No. That's not it at all.'

'What is it then?'

Bryce looked uncomfortable. 'It's just that you're so nice, that's all.'

Cindy laughed softly. 'What does that mean?'

Bryce stuttered. 'You're a nice girl. I mean, you are more like a girl than, say, Sally.'

Cindy chuckled. 'I am no more of a girl than Sally.'

Bryce shrugged and looked away. 'Yeah. But you know what I mean.'

Cindy reached over and touched his arm. 'Are you trying to tell me that you like me?'

Bryce was embarrassed. 'No. I mean, of course I like you.' He added, 'But everyone knows you like Adam.'

'I do like Adam, that's true. But that doesn't mean I can't like you as well.'

Bryce seemed surprised. 'Really?'

'Sure. Bryce, what else are you trying to say to me?'

'Nothing.'

'Are you sure?'

'Yes,' he said.

'I don't believe you.'

'Why don't you believe me?'

'Because I think you like me.'

'I do like you. I just told you that I liked you. What are you asking me?'

Cindy turned away, feeling disappointed for a reason she couldn't pinpoint.

'I don't know,' she said. 'It's nothing. I'm sorry I brought it up.'

Bryce seemed to relax. 'Don't be sorry. I'm the one who brought it up.'

'Whatever it is,' Cindy muttered.

'Yeah. Whatever it is.'

Then they both burst out laughing.

That may have been a mistake, making so much noise.

Too late they realized there were two figures behind them.

And neither of them was wearing skin.

Bony fingers wrapped around their throats. They didn't even have a chance to stand. Over their shoulders smooth white skulls came into view. They heard a sickening hissing sound, felt the cold breath of the grave on their cheeks.

'We want Watch,' hissed the one who was holding Cindy.

Its grip was so tight, she could hardly breathe.

'I don't know where he is,' she gasped.

It tightened its grip. 'You lie, you die,'

Cindy began to choke. Bryce spoke quickly.

'We can take you to his house,' he said.

The skeletons loosened their grips.

'No tricks,' said the one who had been holding Bryce. It sounded vaguely female, as the one that had grabbed Cindy sounded vaguely male. Yet when Cindy and Bryce stood up and turned, they could not tell them apart. They both looked like the most horrifying of creatures, walking death. The skeletons pointed at them with their bony fingers.

'Take us to Watch,' they said together. 'Or you die.'

Bryce didn't even make a grab for his shovel. He could see they were serious. He could see it in the emptiness of their hollow eyes. He decided then he would take them to Watch's house, and stall for time.

It did not seem like such a smart plan when they finally reached Watch's house. Because naturally Watch was not at home, and there was no hiding that fact. The two skeletons pushed Cindy and Bryce into the house and forced them to sit down on the living-room sofa. One of the monsters stood guard while the other searched the house. Cindy was surprised at how little furniture Watch had in his house. She commented on the fact to Bryce.

'I think he lives a rather Spartan existence,' Bryce said.

'He doesn't even have a TV,' Cindy said.

Bryce nodded to the skeleton standing four feet in front of them.

'With visitors like this, who needs the sci-fi channel?' he said.

Now that they had some light, they could see that the skeleton who stood over them was slightly shorter than the other, and wore a tattered dress as opposed to ripped trousers. It even had on a dull gold watch; it – she – must have been buried with it. Cindy could not help but feel sad thinking that this had once been a young girl, probably not much older than herself.

'What's your name?' she asked gently.

'Silence,' it hissed.

'We are not your enemy,' Bryce said.

The skeleton stepped closer and held out a clawed hand.

'Give us Watch,' it said. 'Or die.'

The other skeleton came back into the living-room. It looked angry, if such a thing were possible without any facial skin. Its voice, though, definitely sounded annoyed.

'There is no Watch here,' it – he – hissed.

'He should be home soon,' Bryce said. 'Why don't you two pull up a chair and make yourselves comfortable?'

The male skeleton suddenly stepped forward and grabbed Bryce by the throat. Its grip was intense; Bryce immediately began to turn blue.

'Watch,' he hissed. 'Give us Watch or you die.'

'Stop that!' Cindy screamed, trying to shove it off her friend. 'Who do you think you are? You cannot just choke him. Stop! This is not a monster mash!'

Cindy half expected the other skeleton to attack her.

But it stood very still, as if stunned.

'I like that song,' she hissed.

The skeleton that was choking Bryce paused.

'You know that song?' he hissed.

'Yes,' Bryce gasped.

The boy skeleton released Bryce.

'What other songs do you know?' he asked.

Cindy and Bryce stared at each other in wonder.

The Top Forty certainly survived the years.

It looked like music even survived the grave.

'They must have died in the Sixties,' Cindy said.

Bryce nodded slowly, his colour returning.

'They must still remember it fondly,' he said, turning back to the skeletons. 'Do you guys know the Beach Boys?'

They nodded. 'Surfing USA,' the girl said.

'Surfer Girl,' the guy said.

Cindy leaned forward. 'I have heard Watch say that he has a bunch of old records. Would you two like to hear some of your favourite tunes before you go looking for him some more?'

They nodded. 'Elvis,' the girl said.

'A Hard Day's Night,' the guy said.

Cindy squealed with pleasure. 'You guys know the Beatles?'

They nodded. 'Rock and roll,' the girl said. 'The Stones.'

'I Can't Get No Satisfaction,' the guy said.

Their voices improved as they talked about their favourite songs.

Cindy ran into the other room to dig up some oldies but goodies. Of course she preferred – given their unusual company – not to think that she was digging up anything old. She just hoped she could figure out how to use Watch's record player. The only thing she knew about was CDs. Now wouldn't those blow the skeletons' minds. She seriously considered inviting them home to her own bedroom.

Six

The others were not faring as well. Looking out of the castle window, they saw that they were slowly surrounded by an army of living dead. None of the skeletons had so far tried to cross the moat but Adam, Sally and Watch knew it was only a matter of time. Staring down at the sea of bones, Adam thought that he had never felt such despair. They had come for his friend, come to take him away to the land of the dead. Adam did not know what he could do but he swore to himself that he would do something.

'Is there any way to drive them off?' Adam asked.

'There is no point,' Ann Templeton said. 'They are mere servants. They have come to take Watch to their master. If they are unable to deliver him, then he himself will come.'

'The Grim Reaper would come here?' Sally asked anxiously.

'Yes,' Ann Templeton said.

'You'd better surrender yourself then,' Sally said to Watch.

'Sally!' Adam snapped at her.

'I don't want to give him up any more than you do,' Sally said. 'Neither do I want to meet the Grim Reaper.' She paused and then spoke to Ann Templeton. 'Are you sure there is nothing you can do for my scratch?'

'I have hydrogen peroxide in the kitchen.'

'Is that it?' Sally asked, dismayed.

'You have a scratch, nothing more,' Ann Templeton said.

'Oh,' Sally said. 'I knew it.'

The deathly crowd began to hiss.

'They're getting impatient,' Ann Templeton said.

Watch nodded. 'I should go down.'

'No!' Adam cried. 'You're not going out there. They'll kill you.'

'I believe they will bring him before the Grim Reaper before they kill him,' Ann Templeton said.

'Why?' Adam asked.

'To judge him,' Ann Templeton said. 'To find him guilty of cheating death.'

'Then they will kill me?' Watch asked quietly.

Ann Templeton nodded. 'Then you will be taken away.'

'But there must be something we can do,' Adam pleaded.

Ann Templeton shook her head and she looked genuinely distressed.

'I don't know what to do, really I don't,' she said.

Watch turned. 'It's hopeless. You guys stay here, I will go with them.'

Sally grabbed his arm. 'Don't be so brave. You are not going out there.'

Watch flashed her a faint smile. 'If I thought you could talk the Grim Reaper out of wanting me, then

I would invite you to come with me. But I think that is beyond even your abilities.'

Sally reached out and hugged him. There were tears in her eyes.

'I am not afraid of him,' she said. 'If you must go out there, I'm going with you.'

Watch was touched by her gesture. 'You can't be serious?'

Sally nodded and dried her eyes. 'But I am serious. You should know your friends by now. We're not going to leave you.'

'No way,' Adam said.

Ann Templeton touched Watch's shoulder.

'And I am also your friend,' she said. 'I will go with you as well, and do what I can for you. I am only sorry that I can promise you nothing. Finally we have both met a match beyond our power.'

Watch stared at them all in wonder.

'Your love is the greatest power,' he said with feeling.

Ann Templeton patted him on the back.

'That is a great truth,' she said. 'Is there anything

you want before we go down?'

'One thing,' Watch said. 'Before the army of the dead takes me away, tell them I want to get a few things at my house.'

'What do you want?' Adam asked.

'I just want to go home, that's all,' Watch said. 'Just for a couple of minutes.'

Ann Templeton nodded. 'You shall have your wish. I shall insist upon it.'

At Watch's house, the party was heating up. Cindy had found a bunch of early Beatles and Stones records and had figured out how to work Watch's record player. She could not believe how primitive it was to use a needle to pick up the second. The hissing noise the creaky stereo made must have driven Watch crazy, she thought. But it didn't matter, the skeletons were in seventh heaven, no pun intended.

The skeletons had even started to dance with each other in the middle of the floor when Cindy put on the Stones' *High Tide Green Grass* album.

The dead kids looked like they were finally getting some satisfaction after a hard day's night. It was sort of weird to watch them flailing about, ready at any moment to fall apart. But if you can't beat them join them, so the old saying went. Cindy and Bryce had begun to dance as well. Cindy had never known Bryce was such a skilled dancer and complimented him on his moves.

'I often dance by myself late at night,' Bryce said.

'Why don't you call me up sometime and I'll come over and join you,' Cindy said.

Bryce blinked. 'You would do that?'

'Sure.'

'But wouldn't Adam get mad?'

'Why should Adam get mad?' she asked.

'You know. Because he likes you.'

'If he likes me he's never told me. Look, Bryce, Adam doesn't own me. I don't know where you got that idea. I'm a free spirit.' She glanced at the skeletons. 'Oops, I have to watch what I'm saying.'

'Say what you want,' the girl skeleton called out,

grinding hips, literally, with her partner. 'This is a free country.'

'It's a rocking country,' the guy said, taking a dangerous – by mortal standards – dip. They were actually better dancers than any mortal could be. They had so much less *stuff* to get in the way of their cool moves.

'Hey,' Bryce called over the music. 'What are your names?'

'I'm Sue,' the girl skeleton said.

'I'm Rocky,' the guy said. 'Who are you?'

'I'm Cindy and this is Bryce. How old are you guys? I mean, how old were you when you . . . you know, stopped getting any older?'

'I was fifteen,' Sue said. 'Rocky was sixteen. He had just got his driver's licence.'

'That's how we bit the dust,' Rocky said. 'Never drink and drive.'

'What happened?' Bryce asked.

Sue giggled. 'He drove off the end of the pier!'

'It was a wild Friday night,' Rocky agreed. 'Sort of like tonight. Love this album. Hey, does that

Watch guy have the Everly Brothers' last album?'

'I don't know, I'll have to check,' Cindy said, moving to do so.

But she never got the chance.

The front door swung open.

Cindy was startled. She saw her friends, accompanied by Ann Templeton. That was OK, that she could live with, even though the witch's eyes seemed to shine like alien emeralds. But standing silently behind them was an army of skeletons. Several carried burning torches, their empty eye sockets seemingly sparkling with the light of the flames. Without meaning to, she backed up and bumped into the record player. The needle skipped and the music went off. An icy silence filled the house. From the look on her friends' faces, things were not going well.

'Is it bad?' she asked Watch. Of course she knew it was him they wanted. Watch nodded gravely.

'It cannot get any worse,' he said as he stepped into the house. 'For me.'

Cindy ran to him and hugged him.

'What do they want with you?' she asked, burying her face in his chest.

'They want me to die,' Watch said.

Cindy pulled back from him, searching for a joke in his face, but there was none. Hot tears burned her eyes.

'No,' she said. 'Tell me it isn't true?'

'Watch, get your things,' Ann Templeton said quietly. 'They will not wait much longer.'

'I understand,' Watch said as he let go of Cindy and headed for the back room. Cindy turned to the others.

'How can this happen?' she begged.

Ann Templeton sighed. 'It's like a tale that never ends. It happens again and again.'

'But can't you stop them?' Cindy asked.

Ann Templeton glanced at the waiting skeletons.

'I am thinking,' she said. She glanced back the way Watch had gone, to the rear of the house and added, 'I am not the only one.'

Seven

The doorway to the Grim Reaper's realm was in the cemetery, which was no big surprise to the gang. But the way it suddenly appeared in the ground, not far from Madeline Templeton's and Watch's graves was shocking. The skeletons were leading them into the graveyard and suddenly a square black hole opened before them. Thin steps glowing with a faint silver light led deep into the earth. The skeletons didn't have to push them forward: the dead were crowding so tight at their back, there was nowhere else for them to go.

Watch walked up front with Ann Templeton,

carrying a black suitcase in his right hand. None of them understood why he would pack to go to his own funeral. The others brought up the rear, with two skeletons staying close to Cindy and Bryce. Indeed, to both Adam and Sally's amazement, Cindy and Bryce appeared to be on good terms with the skeletons.

'Sally, Adam,' Cindy said. 'Meet Sue and Rocky.'

The skeletons offered their bony hands.

Adam shook them but Sally declined.

'Pleased to meet you both,' Sue said.

'Too bad our party got interrupted,' Rocky said.

'You guys were having a party?' Adam asked in amazement.

'It's been a long time since we rocked and rolled,' Rocky said.

'How has music changed since the Sixties?' Sue asked.

'It's gotten infinitely worse,' Sally muttered.

'Then it's good we died when we did,' Rocky said.

'But the Stones are still together,' Sally said

gamely. 'But a lot of people say Keith Richard looks like he died a long time ago. He can still play the guitar, though, and I guess that's all that matters.'

'I would like to talk music with you guys,' Adam said with a trace of impatience. 'But do all of you realize who we're going to see?'

Sue nodded. 'The Boss Man.'

'That's one serious dude,' Rocky added.

'Who is it?' Bryce demanded.

Sally spoke in a whisper. 'The Grim Reaper.'

Cindy cringed. 'Oh no. Sue, Rocky, can't you pull some strings for our friend, Watch?'

They both shook their skulls.

'No one argues with the Boss Man,' Rocky said.

'He has no sense of humour,' Sue said.

'But in his line of work it is to be expected,' Rocky said.

'I don't understand,' Bryce said. 'Why does the Grim Reaper want Watch?'

'He feels Watch cheated death when he died during our dangerous quest and then got to keep on living,' Adam explained.

Bryce nodded. 'I can see that.'

Cindy poked him in the side. 'Don't say that in front of all these skeletons.' She spoke to Adam and Sally. 'Can't the witch use her powers on the Grim Reaper?'

Adam sighed. 'She says she can't.'

They had stopped their descent and emerged into a large black cavern whose walls could not even be seen. The army of skeletons spread out all around them. Up ahead the gang could see the faint outline of a silver throne. As they drew closer they became aware of a dark-clad figure sitting on the kingly seat. He was tall but wore a black hood over his head, which cast a thick shadow that hid his face. Closing to within thirty feet, they saw that his hands were long and bony like those of a skeleton. On each wrist he wore a thick silver bracelet that shone with a cold light.

The skeletons lined up on each side of the throne, keeping a respectful distance. Even Sue and Rocky left Cindy and Bryce to join their partners in death, after wishing them good luck, of course. Ann

Templeton was bold. Taking Watch's hand, she approached to within a few feet of the Grim Reaper's throne. They heard him draw in a thin hissing breath at the sight of the witch. He raised a bony finger and pointed at her. For the first time they heard him speak, and his words could have been made of death. His tone was like a whisper lost on a haunted breeze.

'I know you,' he said slowly. 'There will be none of your tricks.'

Ann Templeton nodded. 'We are not here to lie but to talk.'

The Grim Reaper sat up. Still, they could not see his face.

'The time for talking has passed,' he said. 'This young man, this Watch, has tried to cheat death. That is unacceptable.'

'But as the judge of the dead, surely you must listen to his case,' Ann Templeton said. 'That is why I have come, to plead it for him.'

The Grim Reaper sat back. 'You may speak, I will listen.'

'Not that it will make any difference,' Sally muttered. The remainder of the gang hung back, for the moment leaving matters in the hands of Ann Templeton. As she took another step forward, she let go of Watch's hand.

'Watch did not deliberately try to cheat death,' she said in a firm voice. 'It is only by virtue of an accident of time travel that there ended up being two of him. Watch made no bargain with you or anyone else that he did not keep. While on a dangerous quest in another dimension, he genuinely offered his life to save a princess. And he did die, he had to go through the pain of death. That pain alone should be enough to meet your balance of life and death.'

'It does not,' the Grim Reaper said without hesitation. 'Because only a body died. I was not allowed to collect his spirit. Balance has not been achieved.'

'The rules of balance are different in this case,' Ann Templeton said. 'As I mentioned, Watch's other body died in another dimension. His death there should not influence matters here.'

'He gave up his life,' the Grim Reaper said flatly. 'He cannot give it up and still have it. Your argument does not impress me as valid.'

'Then consider how many times Watch has risked his life to save others,' Ann Templeton persisted. 'By doing so he has earned tremendous merit. Enough merit, I would think, to have you overlook the paradox of his two bodies caused by the paradox of the time travel.'

'There is no merit great enough for a mortal to be allowed to cheat death,' the Grim Reaper replied.

A note of anxiety entered Ann Templeton's voice.

'You said you would listen to our case,' she said. 'You dismiss everything I say.'

'Because you are unconvincing,' the Grim Reaper said. 'Watch must die for balance to be achieved. The balance between the living and dead is my domain. That is all that interests me.'

Ann Templeton was angry. 'Did stealing Cio from me bring balance?'

The Grim Reaper raised his hand and pointed another finger.

'Your friend made a bargain with me. I kept my end of the bargain.'

'So did she.'

'Not willingly,' the Grim Reaper said.

'But you took advantage of her grief,' Ann Templeton said.

'I am the Lord of Death. Grief is all I see. Cio knew what she was doing when she made her offer.'

Ann Templeton lowered her voice. 'To this day I am not sure you did not try to cheat her into the bargain.'

The Grim Reaper seemed to shake with anger. His voice came out like a gust of dead air. They all involuntarily took a step back.

'Watch what you say to me lest you come to me before your time,' he warned.

To their surprise his comment made Ann Templeton smile. Yet it was a cold smile, and as she turned and glanced at Watch, the rest of the gang worried what she had in mind. In that moment she looked truly witchy, capable of hatching the most frightening of plots. It was almost as if she had goaded him into saying what he just did. Yet the gang had to wonder who was trying to fool who. Ann Templeton turned back to the Grim Reaper.

'What if I do come to you before my time?' she asked.

The dark cavern grew very still. Even the skeletons seemed to draw in a breath that they somehow held in their hollow chests. The Grim Reaper sat up once more and leaned forward.

'What are you offering?' he asked. He sounded curious.

'My offer is simple,' Ann Templeton said. 'Watch is in this situation because he offered his life to save another life. Very well, I offer my life to save his.'

The gang gasped. The skeletons hissed.

'No,' Watch whispered.

'Be silent,' Ann Templeton snapped at him.

'Why do you do this?' the Grim Reaper asked the witch.

'My reasons are my own,' Ann Templeton said.

'But I know you would rather have my great power than the life of this young man.'

The Grim Reaper considered. 'You tried to trick me once before. I do not trust you, Ann Templeton. You have many years still left to you, and it is true that you have great power. Your destiny is said to be profound. Yet you are willing to throw this all away to save this boy? You must have some other motivation for making this offer.'

Ann Templeton lowered her head. 'This boy is very dear to me. Have you lived so long beneath the earth, in darkness, that you do not understand the ways of the human heart?'

'You are a witch,' the Grim Reaper said.

'I am a witch and a human being,' Ann Templeton replied sharply. 'Do you accept my offer or not? I will argue with you no more.'

The Grim Reaper was silent for a long time. Once more Watch tried to speak to Ann Templeton but she would not listen to him. It was only then that Adam noticed Watch slowly unzipping his black suitcase. There was something coloured inside, sort of doll-shaped. Adam could not imagine what it could be.

Finally the Grim Reaper spoke. His voice was ice.

'I accept your offer, Ann Templeton,' he said. 'On one condition. You must take a vow that you will not try to cheat me out of this bargain. You must swear on something most dear to you.'

Ann Templeton nodded. 'I have already made it clear to you how much this young man means to me. I tell you to your face, O Grim Reaper. On the body of my friend that now lies in Spooksville's cemetery, I swear to you that I now exchange my life for his life.'

Once again the dark cavern was deathly silent. Yet even the army of skeletons seemed moved by the witch's offer. Perhaps the same could be said for even the Grim Reaper. They still could not see his face but two points of silver light suddenly shone within the shadow cast by his black hood. He raised a bony hand and placed it over his chest.

'Now I swear to you, Ann Templeton,' he said. 'I accept your life in exchange for Watch's. He is now free to go.' He removed his hand from his chest and pointed a finger at her. 'But from this moment on you are mine. There is no escape for you.'

Suddenly many things happened at once.

Watch sprung open his suitcase all the way.

He pulled out a funny-looking mechanical doll.

'Stand next to me you guys!' he shouted at them.

They didn't know what he was up to but they did what he said. In a moment they were by Watch's side. Yet he was already on the move, stepping forward to grab Ann Templeton by the arm. She did not seem surprised by his act nor did she resist him. At the same time, however, an angry looking Grim Reaper jumped up from his throne. He stabbed out his left arm and his silver bracelet shone with a sickening light.

'No tricks!' he commanded.

Then there came another flash of light. But this light was white, and somehow familiar to the rest of the gang. The dark cavern vanished and they felt as if they were falling. Not down but outwards, to the far end of the universe and back. It seemed as if stars spun all around them and they entered a place where time and even life and death had no meaning. Then all went black for a length of time they could not even imagine.

Eight

When they became aware of their surroundings once more they were standing on a dark deserted plain. Overhead there were a few stars in a black sky but they looked faint and far away. Burned out, even, as if they had long ago exhausted their precious fuel on youthful glories. They did not even seem to sparkle.

The plain was relatively featureless. There were smooth rolling hills but no signs of life. No trees or bushes or grass. Even the air seemed empty, it was sort of hard to breathe. They had to struggle to draw in enough oxygen.

They could not imagine where they could be.

Yet the answer was very simple, and totally confusing.

'Where are we?' Sally gasped. They could barely see each other.

'Spooksville,' Watch said softly, in the dark. He still seemed to be holding on to the strange-looking toy. 'Ten billion years in the future.'

Adam sucked in a breath. 'You used the Time Toy to teleport us.'

'To teleport us in time, not in space,' Watch explained. 'In reality we have gone nowhere.' He turned to the witch, who stood silently, staring up at the stars. 'You knew I brought it with me?'

Yet Ann Templeton seemed distracted.

'If this the future of our galaxy?' she whispered to herself. 'A place with dying stars? I never imagined it would end this way.'

'Ten billion years is a long time,' Watch said gently.

She finally looked at him. 'Why did you take us so far?'

'I wanted to make sure he couldn't follow us,' Watch said.

Ann Templeton returned to staring at the stars.

'It was a clever move,' she said. 'I am grateful.'

Watch spoke with rare emotion. 'I am grateful to you for offering your life for mine.'

Without looking Ann Templeton reached over and rubbed his head.

'It was the least I could do,' she said. But then her voice dropped. 'He will find us here eventually. I have tried this before. One cannot cheat death easily.'

'But you tried to escape in space,' Watch protested. 'He will not think to search for us this far in the future.'

Ann Templeton shook her head as she drew back her hand.

'He knows you possessed a time travel device. That is how all this trouble started in the first place. Once he has searched the local galaxy his attention will turn to the future and to the past. He has tremendous powers. As I said, eventually he will find us.'

'Then where can we hide?' Adam asked.

'We can't.' Ann Templeton lowered her head. 'I can't.'

'But we can't leave you,' Watch said. 'We won't, not after you have tried so hard to help us.'

'Well, we could leave,' Sally muttered. 'I do have to get home soon.'

'Your home turned to dust billions of years ago,' Bryce said seriously. 'All you ever knew is dead and buried.'

'A little less gloomy, Bryce, please,' Cindy said.

'Sorry,' Bryce said.

'Yeah,' Sally said. 'Since we still have the Time Toy, we can go anywhere in time.' She paused. 'Can't we?'

'Yes,' Watch said. 'As far as I know.'

'You have to go back,' Ann Templeton said. 'Your lives are there.' She gestured to the deserted plain. They only realized then that even the ocean was gone. Long ago, it must have been, it had dried up on the dry wind that blew faintly across the plain. The witch added, 'There is no life here.'

'Then you can't stay here either,' Watch said.

Ann Templeton nodded. 'I know.'

'But if you go back the Grim Reaper will get you right away,' Adam said. 'You will die. Why don't we keep shifting in time? Try to throw him off our track?'

Ann Templeton shook her head. 'You are not listening to me. I made the deal I did with the Grim Reaper so that you could all have your lives back. And those lives lie back in time. None of us can try to escape by hopping around into other people's worlds. That is not right. It is not your destiny.'

Watch sounded sad. 'Then you will die?' he asked.

Once again Ann Templeton stared up at the stars.

'I tried to save Cio and Sam by running away into outer space,' she said. 'Looking back, I see that it was a childish kind of escape. But for our present situation, I see that that might not have been a bad thing. I am sure that the Grim Reaper expects much the same from me again. I think that is why he was not afraid to bargain with me.'

'But he seemed reluctant,' Adam said.

Ann Templeton lowered her head and looked at them.

'That is not true,' she said. 'From the moment we entered his throne room, probably even before then, he had his eyes fixed on me. He is still mad at me for trying what I did with Cio and Sam. I hope to use that anger against him.' She paused. 'And maybe I already have.'

'I don't understand.' Adam said.

'I think I do,' Watch said, staring at her.

Ann Templeton gestured to Watch.

'Come,' she said. 'I have to talk to you in private. Before you all return, I have to have you send me to a certain point in time.'

'But I want to know what is going on,' Sally complained. 'We do things together in this gang.'

Ann Templeton smiled at Sally. 'If I tell you what I am going to do and you return and stand before the Grim Reaper he will probably cut off your head and pry out your brains and try to get the information out of you that way.'

Sally took a step back. 'In that case I don't mind if you two have a nice private conversation.'

Watch and Ann Templeton went off a little way in the dark. They spoke quietly so that no one else could hear. The rest of the gang huddled together. They were still having trouble breathing but they were getting used to it. Yet it was sad, the seeming desolation of the Earth. It was as if all of humanity had just faded into the dust at their feet.

'I wonder what became of all the people,' Bryce said wistfully.

'Probably aliens attacked the Earth and captured all the people and brought them back to their home world and ate them,' Sally said.

'That's a cheerful view of the future,' Adam remarked.

It was Cindy's turn to stare up at the sky.

'Maybe they went to the stars long ago,' she said. 'Maybe they met wonderful creatures there who taught them how to become perfect. Something greater than simple people, but people still, that we would still recognize and love.'

'What a beautiful thought,' Adam said.

'I hope that is what did happen,' Bryce agreed.

'I consider it highly unlikely,' Sally muttered.

They saw a flash of white light off to their right.

Carrying the Time Toy, Watch slowly walked back to them.

Even in the poor light they could see that he was worried.

'Where did she go?' Sally asked.

'Back to Spooksville,' Watch said.

'*When* did she go?' Bryce asked, the more important question.

Watch hesitated. 'Not long after we left.'

'That was foolish,' Bryce said. 'The Grim Reaper will grab her in a few minutes.'

'Ann Templeton is never foolish,' Watch snapped. Then he lowered his voice. 'A few minutes is a long time for her. She can do much.'

'What will she do?' Cindy asked.

Watch wound up the Time Toy.

'We will see,' he said. 'Prepare yourselves. We are also going back.'

'To when?' Adam asked as they moved closer to Watch.

But Watch was already walking away, to another spot. Adam understood what he was doing. They were standing on Spooksville. Watch wanted to return to their time, but in a different part of town. The rest of them followed him but they still had many questions. Adam just hoped Watch and the witch had figured out a smart plan.

'We are also going back to the same time,' Watch said.

'Oh no,' Sally moaned.

'We have to,' Watch said seriously. 'There is no running from death.'

Yet his voice was not defeated.

Watch and Ann Templeton had something up their sleeve.

Nine

They materialized back in Spooksville close to the pier, by the water. Ocean Avenue was deserted. No one really went out after dark in Spooksville – unless they were crazy – and it was clearly long after the sun had set. Watch quickly checked one of his four watches.

'When are we?' Adam asked

'Two hours after we left,' Watch said.

'Is that good?' Sally wanted to know.

'I hope so,' Watch said.

'Where is Ann Templeton?' Bryce asked.

'We shall see,' Watch said evasively. He looked

up and down the street. 'We've got to make some noise.'

'What?' Cindy asked.

'Do you want to attract the skeletons' attention?' Adam asked.

Watch nodded. 'Exactly.'

Cindy and Bryce exchanged a knowing look.

'If you want to get their attention we know just the thing,' Cindy said.

'Yeah.' Bryce agreed. 'I think a lot of these guys died in the Sixties. That was a rough decade for the country as a whole but especially in this town. Let's get back to your house, Watch, put on a few oldies but goodies and crank up your stereo real loud. Believe me they will come a-running.'

'This night is getting weirder by the minute,' Sally muttered.

'What do we do when the skeletons arrive?' Adam asked.

'Surrender,' Watch said.

'But they might want to kill us all,' Sally said. 'And steal your records while they're at it.'

'They might,' Watch said.

Yet at Watch's house they were surprised to find Sue and Rocky already there, dancing in the centre of the living-room to an old Elvis album. They waved as the gang came bursting through the door but they did not stop dancing. They were getting wilder with their moves; their bones were practically cracking into each other.

'Where did you guys go?' Rocky asked. He sounded out of breath which was odd because he did not seem to be breathing. Certainly he didn't have any lungs.

'Into the future,' Cindy said.

'Cool,' Sue said.

'You know we still use that word in our time,' Bryce said. 'It has made a come back, of sorts.'

'Totally cool,' Sue said. They had both changed their clothes. Sue was wearing a red short skirt and Rocky had on blue bell-bottoms and a bright coloured shirt. The gang could only imagine where the skeletons had got the clothes from.

Watch stepped over to the stereo. It was up loud but not too loud.

'What are you guys doing here?' Watch asked.

'Having a party,' Rocky said.

'But we're supposed to be searching for you,' Sue explained. 'The Boss Man sent us out to find you and drag you back to his dark throne.'

'Doesn't that just beat all,' Sally muttered.

'Are you going to take us back?' Cindy asked.

Both the skeletons shrugged, and it was an interesting gesture since they were nothing but bones. Yet the tiny bones on their faces showed emotion as well. Clearly they did not want to obey the Grim Reaper.

'It's possible that we could say that we never saw you,' Rocky said.

'Yeah,' Sue agreed. 'Or you could just leave now and we can forget that we saw you.'

Watch shook his head as he fiddled with his stereo.

'I want the whole army of you guys to come running to this house,' he said. 'For that reason I am

108

going to have to turn off the music for a few minutes. But don't worry, I will turn it back on when I have hooked up a few extra-large speakers that I am going to place on my front porch.'

'That sounds like a block party!' Rocky exclaimed.

'Oh that would be so cool!' Sue said. 'We haven't been to a block party since the night we died.'

'And that was one heck of a party,' Rocky said. 'But I do want to state clearly before it gets going that I don't want anyone drinking and driving. I have learned my lesson in that area.'

'Especially drinking and driving off the end of a pier,' Sue added. 'Hey, I wonder if our car is still there? What do you think, Rocky? Down there in the seaweed with all the little fish?'

'I wouldn't mind checking it out,' Rocky said.

'Cool,' Sue said again.

Watch turned off the record and began to pull out the wires at the back of the stereo. 'I don't want you guys to leave just yet. I need you to stand out on the porch and welcome all your fellow skeletons as they come to the party. But don't tell them at first that we are here. We'll hide in the back room. But when the place is real crowded, we'll suddenly show ourselves.'

'They'll grab you and drag you off to the Boss Man,' Rocky warned.

'He wants to know where that witch is,' Sue said. 'He's real mad at her, man. I've never seen him so upset. You're going to have to tell him where she is or you'll end up worse than us.'

'What could be worse?' Sally muttered.

Rocky smiled at her with his white skull face.

'You would be amazed,' he said.

The army of skeletons gathered quickly. With the music blaring out over the city and the gang hiding in a back room, Adam and Watch peered out of a window and watched as the bony creatures poured into the block party. They had put on a Beatles album. They figured there was no way they could lose with that.

Naturally no *real* people came to the party. The

town police did not even stop by to see what all the noise was about. Probably one look at all the wandering skeletons and nobody mortal dared go outside. Of course it was just another night in Spooksville – business as usual.

Sue and Rocky made great hosts. They invited all the skeletons inside and pushed the furniture aside and made everyone feel welcome. Actually having a party for the dead saved a lot of trouble. No one had to worry about what they would eat because they didn't have any stomachs.

When the house was filled to capacity, Watch stood and said it was time to reveal themselves. The others still did not understand what he was up to, although Adam had an idea.

'Why don't we just sneak out the back way?' Sally asked.

'No,' Watch said flatly.

'But I don't want to see that Boss Man again,' Cindy complained. 'He gives me the creeps.'

'But you acted bravely in front of him,' Bryce said.

Cindy smiled. 'Thank you. You also acted very brave, Bryce. I was proud of you.'

Sally stared at them in wonder. 'What is going on here?' she demanded.

Cindy squeezed Bryce's arm. 'We have just got to know each other better, that's all.'

Sally turned to Adam. 'Don't you have anything to say about this type of disgusting behaviour?'

But Adam was preoccupied with their immediate crisis.

'This has all been an elaborate distraction,' Adam said to Watch. 'You have just been trying to keep the Grim Reaper's skeleton forces busy so that Ann Templeton can do something else?'

Watch looked away. 'She asked me not to talk about her plan. But I can say we have to reveal ourselves now, before it gets any later.'

Adam nodded. 'Because we are the main distraction.'

'It sounds to me like we're the main sacrifice,' Sally grumbled.

There was no arguing with Watch. He stepped to

the door and threw it open and shouted out to the party skeletons. They took a moment to notice him and the others, then the music suddenly died. Party or no party most of them apparently knew that it was not a good idea to anger the Boss Man. The gang was grabbed and dragged out on to the street. None of them were surprised to see that they were being pushed back towards the cemetery.

Where it had all begun.

And now where it might all end.

Ten

The Grim Reaper was not waiting for them on his dark throne beneath the earth. He must have been extremely anxious to question them. He met them out on the road not far from the cemetery. He had obviously been hunting for them himself. But he had not thought to look in the very place where all his forces had gathered.

Perhaps he had not thought to look in another obvious place.

For Ann Templeton. It was clear it was she he wanted.

Perhaps it had been his plan from the very beginning, as she suspected. Watch might have just been an excuse. Adam was beginning to think so.

The gang was forced to their knees by the skeletons who held them. Sue and Rocky were lost somewhere in the crowd and these skeletons were not friendly. They were all wearing tattered police uniforms and Adam finally understood why Watch had been worried about that from the start. The leaders of the dead had been leaders while they were alive. From the beginning, Watch must have suspected that the dead had a powerful leader behind them who used lesser authority figures to control the bulk of the skeletons.

The Grim Reaper seemed to tower over them.

'Where is she?' he demanded.

'We don't know,' Sally said.

The Grim Reaper pointed an angry finger at her. 'You lie,' he said.

Sally made a face. 'Gimme a break. Why would that witch tell me where she was going? We're not even friends.'

The Grim Reaper stared at her with his silver

eyes and then suddenly his attention went to Watch. It was as if he could pick up a few of their thoughts. But not all their thoughts – he still needed their help to catch Ann Templeton. He bore down on Watch, holding his shadowed face only inches from Watch's nose.

'If you do not tell me where she is,' he warned. 'You will once more have to take her place.'

Watch looked scared but still in control of himself.

'That was not the deal you struck with her,' Watch said.

The Grim Reaper hissed. 'You dare argue with me?'

'I was just stating a fact,' Watch said.

The Grim Reaper stood tall. He was mad.

'It is a fact, if you will recall, that she offered to give her life for yours,' he said. 'I only want what is rightfully mine.'

To their immense surprise Watch brushed off the skeleton hands that held him pinned to the ground and stood up himself. Now all fear seemed to leave him. He spoke with authority to the Grim Reaper.

'You want her so that you can kill her,' Watch said. 'All you know is death, you are such a one dimensional character. But none of us will help you achieve your goal. We are interested in life. Your threats don't scare us. And we love Ann Templeton just as she loves us. The power of that love is what will stop you. Next to that, you are nothing.'

The Grim Reaper gathered himself up to reply.

Actually, he looked on the verge of striking Watch down.

His silver bracelets shone with evil light.

His wicked eyes glittered with hatred.

Yet he froze when a soft voice spoke from the top of the wall that enclosed the cemetery. The wall was just off to the Grim Reaper's right. There stood Ann Templeton in her green dress, Bryce's shovel in her right hand, marks of dirt on both her arms.

'He is right, you know,' she said quietly. She tossed the shovel aside.

The Grim Reaper appeared momentarily confused. Then he mastered himself and stabbed a fleshless finger in her direction.

'You belong to me now!' he shouted.

She smiled. 'You are wrong.' She glanced over her shoulder and they all followed her gaze. In the middle of the cemetery burned a rather large pile of logs. The wood could have been from the broken branches of the many dead trees that persisted in standing in the cemetery. In either case the fire looked like some kind of funeral pyre, which Adam suspected was exactly what it was. He remembered the wording of Ann Templeton's vow to the Grim Reaper.

'*I have already made it clear to you how much this young man means to me. I tell you to your face, O Grim Reaper. On the body of my friend that now lies in Spooksville's cemetery, I swear to you that I now exchange my life for his life.*'

She had made a vow with a special condition attached.

'What have you done?' the Grim Reaper whispered.

119

Ann Templeton laughed softly. 'While you were out searching the far corners of the galaxy for me, and your troops were occupied with my friends. I sneaked into your own backyard and removed the foundation of my vow to you. I told you the truth, Watch is very dear to me. But what lay in the cemetery was not the real Watch. The real Watch is alive, so very much alive. I swore on nothing when I swore on his body and I destroyed nothing when I lifted it into the funeral pyre. But you never suspected that I would do such a thing in the most obvious of places. All because last time I tried to escape I flew to the other end of the universe. All because Watch is right, you are nothing but a dead head, so totally focused on death that you foolishly allowed me to make a vow on something meaningless. Really, you are a one dimensional nuisance.'

The Grim Reaper was silent for a long time. When he finally did speak it was with no strength. His voice was a mere rattle of chains that were old and rusty.

'You cannot do this to me,' he said.

Ann Templeton was strong. 'It is done and your time out in our world is finished. Go back to your dark throne and your gloomy thoughts. You have nothing left to hold over either my head or Watch's.'

The Grim Reaper went to snap at her but then seemed to think better of it. He turned to his assembled skeletons.

'It is time we returned to the ground,' he said quietly.

'Can we bring a Beatles album with us?' a voice shouted out. It sounded like Rocky. The next voice definitely belonged to Sue.

'Shh. Don't get him any madder than he already is.'

The Grim Reaper turned and walked back towards the cemetery entrance. The army of skeletons followed. But as Sue and Rocky passed the gang, they waved and blew kisses. Cindy and Bryce waved back, sad to see them go. Only when they were all gone, all out of sight, did Ann Templeton step down from her place on top of the wall. She went straight to Watch and hugged him. The gang was touched to see that they both had tears in their eyes.

'You did it,' Watch told her.

'No.' She let go of him and messed up his hair. 'You did it, for all of us, but especially for me. By your example, you gave me the courage to give my life for a friend. Now it is true that both our lives have been spared, but if I had had you back when Cio and Sam were alive, things might have turned out different.'

'You did what you could for them,' Watch said gently.

Ann Templeton let go of him and glanced at the funeral pyre that continued to burn inside the cemetery. Then her eyes strayed to the stars above.

'Perhaps you are right,' she replied. 'I don't think Cio's sacrifice for Sam was wasted, or my efforts on their behalf.' She added quietly, probably to herself, as she gazed at the heavens. 'It is good to see so many stars again.'

Spooksville

CHRISTOPHER PIKE

❏	68622 7	Invasion Of The No Ones	£2.99
❏	68623 5	Time Terror	£2.99
❏	68624 3	The Thing In The Closet	£2.99
❏	68625 1	Attack Of The Giant Crabs	£2.99
❏	68626 X	Night Of the Vampire	£2.99

All Hodder Children's books are available at your local bookshop or newsagent, or can be ordered direct from the publisher. Just tick the titles you want and fill in the form below. Prices and availability subject to change without notice.

Hodder Children's Books, Cash Sales Department, Bookpoint, 39 Milton Park, Abingdon, OXON, OX14 4TD, UK. If you have a credit card you may order by telephone – (01235) 831700.

Please enclose a cheque or postal order made payable to Bookpoint Ltd to the value of the cover price and allow the following for postage and packing:
UK & BFPO – £1.00 for the first book, 50p for the second book, and 30p for each additional book ordered up to a maximum charge of £3.00.
OVERSEAS & EIRE – £2.00 for the first book, £1.00 for the second book, and 50p for each additional book.

Name ....

Address ....

....

....

If you would prefer to pay by credit card, please complete:
Please debit my Visa/Access/Diner's Card/American Express (delete as applicable) card no:

Signature ....

ExpiryDate ....